NEW VALHALLA

AHMED ZIADI

CHAPTER 1
THE LAST WAR

When the first atomic bomb fell on Washington, there were already several on their way to Moscow. The decision to respond with nuclear bombs from the Russian side also did not take long to decide on. The presidents from both sides were already heading down to their bunkers when the order to launch the missiles bounced around from officer to officer.

When it was first noticed that the atomic bomb was heading towards the United States, it was immediately assumed that Russia had launched the missile. The relationship between the countries has never been as bad as it was on the sunny doomsday.

The bomb was expected to arrive in Washington for 29 minutes when it was discovered. The President's order was completed 27 minutes before detonation. 5 minutes later, the US had launched 48 missiles at Moscow, St: Petersburg, Novosibirsk, Yekaterinburg and

Kazan and more. There was a calculation of more than 35 million dead in less than a minute. 35 million people who will lose their lives completely unaware.

Russia's response was 33 missiles fired at Washington, New York, Los Angeles, Chicago and several other cities with more than 40 million people living in those cities.

As the news of the missiles reached the other governments around the world, everyone began to look around to see who their allies and enemies are and before the analysis of who launched the attack had come out, more missiles had been launched. Countries that have been waiting for a miracle to arrive began thanking their gods and attacking other countries where an attack has only been in their wildest dreams.

A few hours after the attack, the world was in a full-scale nuclear war with a bomb dropping every minute and millions of people disappearing from the face of the earth. People whose existence is vaporized by the most terrifying weapon created by man.

It wasn't long before the world was in a large-scale war, a war from which we can never recover, a war that murdered the largest part of all people in the world. The last war.

That everything we have accomplished in the past decades will be completely forgotten and our existence will perhaps be completely unknown to those remaining on earth. For the few who escaped unscathed, this day became known as Judgment Day. The day when people will never be the same again.

CHAPTER 2

DOOMSDAY

300 years after the incident or doomsday, the earth has begun to recover. The trees have started to turn green again and our old big cities have been buried by forests. The water has started to flow again. The earth has managed to recover and human existence is barely visible.

The first years after the judgment day have been difficult for man to live in. Hunger and cold everyone thought would be their biggest obstacles. Oh how wrong they were. In the first year alone, more than half of all people who survived the doomsday died. Starvation, no access to clean water and healthcare were problems the world had in poor countries.

Human greed has always been limitless. We could always watch other people die as long as we couldn't relate to them. Now this was not a developing country problem but now it is a global problem and yesterday's poorest countries were better at surviving. People sought out those they used to look down upon. Migrations were reversed. Walls that have been erected to stop migrants from one side to another were taken down for man to migrate back. Cold and hunger became too hard for humans. Time heals all wounds they say, it couldn't be more true. People were welcomed to each other. Doors were opened and houses were divided. For those who remained on this earth, the world became a more open world.

When the people have healed most of their wounds, new societies began to rise up. Most of the survivors sought their way back to the richest continent on earth. The continent that always gives more than it takes. Africa.

In Africa, the largest cities on Earth were built with Lagos as the largest hub for the survivors. A city that has always been looked down upon, Lagos managed to become the capital of the world. With more than 40 million inhabitants, the city became a center for all people on earth with an abundance of food and clean water. A city where all people could live side by side regardless of race, skin color and background. Over time, several cities began to be built and people were able to connect with each other. New roles were created and leaders began to be chosen again. Time passes but old habits remain. After a couple of decades, humans began to find new ways to distinguish themselves. Old habits never die. New human classes were created and divisions between people came back to the surface. Rich, poor, Muslim, Christian, black, white. Old habits never die.

At the northernmost of the northernmost was an island that refused to go back to those old ways. Iceland, which has been one of the least affected by the nuclear weapons, suffered its losses from the cold and famine. With no transport to the island, the people had to suffer. Those who had the opportunity to seek the warmer and greener Lagos did so. Those who couldn't, or for that matter didn't want to, stayed behind. Over the years, people adapted to their new environment. The people went back to their roots and new cities were built. The new city was called New Valhalla. The Nordics' new oasis. The city where the hard-boned Vikings live. They called themselves New Vikings and lived a modest life. Their main concern was living for the day and partying all night.

The town was small, with only 300 inhabitants. Everyone worked from childhood to meet any need that might arise. A primitive life considers residents of Lagos, however, people sought to New Valhalla to get away from Lagos, even though most of them could not stay and went back, life never changed in New Valhalla.

CHAPTER 3
HARALD

Among them New Vikings lived Harald. The cold has made New Vikings wider and harder. Harald was one of the strongest of them. No one could hunt better or live more modestly. No one could party harder than Harald either. During the day, Harald led the hunting party that brought all the supplies to the city's inhabitants. In the evening he was always found in the middle of the party where he was always the focal point of the party.

Harald lived together with his mother Ingrid, who was the town's oldest. Ingrid acted as the city's judge, advisor and problem solver. She was known for her honesty and righteousness.

Although life in New Valhalla was seen as an insignificant and modest life, it did not mean that everyday problems did not exist. Ingrid got to spend her day solving any problems that might arise between the residents. In the evening she sat and waited for Harald to return before she could go to bed. Her only dream was to see Harald become the man who can lead New Valhalla to the heights she has always only dreamed of.

For Harald, Ingrid was more expensive than life itself. She was the most important person in his life and the only person who could always make sure to keep him in check.

Although Ingrid and Harald appeared to be the oddest of them all, they probably had the most harmonious life of all in New Valhalla. With his outgoing and irresponsible lifestyle, he complemented Ingrid's responsible and serious lifestyle. Their roles in the New Vikings were the most critical to the city's well-being and despite the city's lack of a de-facto leader, the two of them were seen as the leaders of New Valhalla and also the New Vikings.

Harald's everyday life began with eating the breakfast that Ingrid always woke up early in the morning to cook for herself and Harald. She always made sure he was fed and satisfied for the daily hunt. Then Harald begins his daily routine of gathering the hunters and going to the Great Forest as he knew by heart, no one in all of New Valhalla was better than Harald at finding his prey. Harald's gift of being able to feel the heartbeats of all creatures in the forest gave him the ability to find his prey. Before Harald could handle his gift, it was difficult for him to distinguish the heartbeats of all creatures where the heartbeats of humans and animals were the same to him. Now at that age, one concentration is enough to feel everyone's heartbeat. That gift meant that he was always in the right place at the right time to help the residents of the city as well as find all the loot in the Great Forest. Despite all these qualities, Harald lived by the code of never hunting more than was required to meet the needs of all the inhabitants.

Harald's dream has always been to protect his city and his people. Having everyone full is just part of making this dream come true. Little did he know that this dream will be much more difficult than that.

CHAPTER 4
CELBERATION

The ancestors of New Vikings set the rules for what it is today. The ancestors were survivors of the doomsday and had seen what a person's greed and evil can accomplish, therefore they decided to create a society where everyone can live, where there are no individuals but everyone should think of the best of everyone. Harald was the very image of their dream.

Every year the city celebrates the day New Vikings came to life. During the celebration, residents spend the day partying from sunrise to the next sunrise. All residents participate in the celebration, children and adults alike. The day before the celebration starts, people start planning for the celebration by preparing a large banquet with the best of the Storskogen and decorating the whole town.

At sunrise, the people begin to wake up to the music playing from the loudspeakers to announce that the celebration has started. It always starts with the kids running out where the family activities are already planned and the kids spend their day socializing and running around between all the activities in town. The adults celebrate the day by drinking the coldest and strongest beer in all of New Valhalla. The beer is stored in the snow for six months to prepare for the celebration, which gives it a special aftertaste that can only be enjoyed once a year.

During the celebration, Ingrid is hoisted down from a hot air balloon by the townspeople to celebrate their chief and give her the gratitude she deserves for her work over the year in making their lives easier and better. Harald also gets his celebration together with his hunters where the first barrel of beer is given to the hunters who make sure that all the inhabitants of the city are full and satisfied. This year's celebration was no different from previous years.

As usual, Harald was waiting for Gjør, who is his best friend and the deputy leader of the hunters. He stood outside his door and looked around at all the children running around in Stortorget. Suddenly he felt a blow on his back and when he turned around he was standing there. Even though Harald is one of the biggest creatures in New Valhalla, he is nowhere near how big and mighty Gjør is. Gjør is related to the ancestors and his family is considered a noble family in New Valhalla but Gjør has never acted like one. Despite his appearance, he behaves more like a teddy bear than a hunter. Lives to laugh and joke and is always the funniest in town. From his childhood, he has always created pranks in the city where nothing or no one could stop him except one person, Ingrid. With her determination, Ingrid has always pushed Gjør into the hunter he is today. Even though the whole town has seen Gjør as a bad influence on Harald, Ingrid has always encouraged their friendship and sensed the brotherhood between these two.

"Thank you old friend for waiting for me" said Gjør with his rough voice and a childish smile on his face. Harald turned around and as soon as he caught sight of his friend, his expression changed from one of surprise to a friendlier but annoyed expression and said "You are always so harsh Gjør". Gjør responded by asgarva for his friend.

Friends started walking towards the crowd to meet their hunters. On the way, the people bowed to them to show their gratitude to the men who ensure that there is food on their plates.

"Do you think the food will be enough today?" asked Do. "Not the way you think," replied Harald with a smile. "What else is there to do in life but eat and have fun" said Gjør with a loud laugh.

When the men arrived at their band, everyone began to eagerly greet their leaders and began to walk towards the crowd to open the first keg of beer.

This year was no different from the previous years and the crowd was as large as every year, adults and children, women and men, everyone gathered in the square to wait for Ingrid to be hoisted down from the hot air balloon with the big beer keg to be opened by

Harald with his axe, the same ax that makes sure there is enough food for the whole city.

"I see the balloon" shouted one of the children loudly and everyone in the crowd began to look up at the sky and cheer loudly for the hot air balloon that appeared to be coming down to the crowd.

It didn't take long for the balloon to arrive before Harald went over to help Ingrid get down from the basket and into the crowd, however to his surprise there was no one in the basket.

With a surprised, he continued to look again to see if he has missed something before he heard a hurried roar behind him to turn around to see the faces of the crowd full of fear and crying. He looked around until he saw the beer keg lying on the ground with a blanket lying next to it, beside his eye caught an arm sticking out. He quickly jumped to the blanket and lifted it to see the last thing he thought he would see, namely Ingrid's dead body.

CHAPTER 5

MOTHER

A couple of days have passed since Ingrid's body was found during the celebration. Gjør and the hunters were on their way to the Great Forest, he stopped halfway and looked back towards the dark house where Harald lives. "Do you think he will hunt with us again?" wondered one hunter looking at another hunter. Gjor turned hastily and told the hunters to be quiet. He took one last look at the house before continuing through the forest with the hunters behind. He wondered when his friend will open the door for him next.

Harald sat on the armchair with the red blanket in his hand. He looks down at it and the tears come uncontrollably. The sight of Ingrid's dead body does not leave his mind and quickly becomes enraged and begins destroying the furniture in the house before breaking down and falling to the floor clutching the blanket tightly with tears refusing to stop falling.

Later in the evening, Harald hears someone knocking on the door. "Harald, open the door my brother" says Gjør who is standing on the other side of the door. Harald continues to sit down on the armchair unmoved. "We need you my friend" continues Gjør, "New Valhalla needs you".

The words from Gjør cause Harald's memories to go back to the day he came back from school and sees the queue outside his home with all the people seeking Ingrid's wisdom. He remembers how he got angry that people always come to his mother with their problems. During dinner he broaches the subject with Ingrid, "How do you cope with all their squishy little problems" he asked her, with a determined look Ingrid replied "No problem is too squishy or small my boy, everyone has their problems, but if I can reduce their burden even if it is a gnarly problem, then my life has meaning". My life has a meaning, Harald thought. The voice from the other side became louder from Gjør, "OPEN HARALD" he continued to say.

Harald walked slowly and opened the door. Gjør stood outside with a smile and a dozen beer bottles and the same childish smile that Harald is used to seeing.

"May I come in" Gjør wondered. Harald just turned around and left the door open. Gjør entered with slow steps and looked around at the wreckage that Harald created a couple of hours ago, the only thing standing intact is the armchair and Ingrid's rocking chair. Gjør gets a lump in his throat when he sees Ingrid's empty chair, he manages his emotions and turns to his friend and says "Today I probably caught the biggest deer ever, you would never have been able to catch it". Harald continues towards armchairs and settles down without looking at Do it once. Gjor sits down on the ground and says "I like the way you have decorated the house, is it a new style?". Harald continues to be dead quiet.

A few seconds pass before Gjør continues "You missed the funeral my brother, it was probably the biggest and grandest funeral ever, everyone was there". Gjor looks at Harald who continues to be unmoved and sitting on the armchair. Gjør opens the caps of two beer bottles and puts one in Harald's hand, then he lifts his bottle and turns to the rocking chair and says quietly "To you Ingrid the righteous, see you in Valhalla" and takes a sip. Harald also takes a sip and lifts his bottle and quickly looks at the empty rocking chair. Gjør sits down on the ground again and the friends drink their bottles in silence while Harald tries to take in all the heartbeats he can sense throughout the city, he wishes to hear Ingrid's heartbeat one last time.

CHAPTER 6
HEARTBEAT

After three weeks, Harald goes back to the hunt, he is received by the hunters and Gjør with hugs and joy. The entire town had come out that day to greet the men and show their support for their leader in the absence of Ingrid, most trying to hide their tears while others didn't even try.

The Great Forest looked bigger than usual to Harald, his steps began to slow as he looked at the place he knew by heart, today it feels like a strange place. Gjør put her arm on his shoulder and asked "Are you okay?", Harald nodded and continued towards the forest.

Inside the forest, old habits began to return and Harald began to close his eyes and take in all the heartbeats he could sense and filter. He quickly pointed to the right and began to run with the hunters behind in steady pace, the deer had no chance of Harald's arrow and fell before it could detect his presence. Gjør got a smile on his face and happily said "Good hunting!", Harald looked at him with a smile. The hunters ran up to the prey and began to wrap it up to take it back to the city. The hunt continued for a couple of hours before Gjør roared "That's enough my brother, we've hunted what we need for today". The men closed their eyes and thanked the forest for the hunt and began to walk back to the city.

The men talked loudly about how good the day's catch was. Harald walked behind silently, surveying the forest as if it was the first time he had done so. He thought about how much he misses the forest and how glad he is to be back before a low mood struck just as quickly and he started thinking about Ingrid again. He heard a shout from Gjør and looked at him, he started to smile and got a smile back and continued walking. He didn't have time to take a step before he felt a loud heartbeat behind him, he turned around suddenly with a startled feeling and felt the heartbeat approaching him at an unnatural speed. Harald took out his ax to meet what was coming at him. He heard Gjør call out and turned to him quickly before turning back and then the heartbeat disappeared.

Gjør ran towards Harald and put his hands on his shoulders and asked "Has something happened my brother?". Harald continued looking around before he could control himself and look at Gjør again and say "N.. No, I thought I heard something, must have heard wrong". "You're getting old my friend" says Gjør and laughs loudly, "Come on, it's getting dark, let's go back before the beer runs out". Harald looks around to try to see the source of the heartbeat however sees the forest as it always has, the heartbeat has completely disappeared. He continues walking behind Gjør and leaves the forest.

Once home, Harald takes a shower and goes to sit in the armchair. He can't stop thinking about the heartbeat as he in the forest. He looks towards the rocking chair and wishes Ingrid was there, she would surely have an answer to what the heartbeat is, he thought. Ingrid always used to say that all creatures on earth are connected and that everything has a meaning. He thought about how different the heartbeat sounded, he usually has to concentrate to feel the different heartbeats, this one was completely different, like it was searching for him, like it was trying to find him himself, he felt a little ashamed because he was scared of it, but thought it must have some meaning.

Harald lay awake all night where the only thing he could think about was his heartbeat. He got up and drank a glass of water, on the way back to his bedroom, he glanced at the rocking chair, he stopped and walked over to it, he put his hand slowly on it and closed his eyes, he saw Ingrid and smiled, he opened eyes with the smile still on his face and turned towards the bedroom. Once at the door, he suddenly heard it. Harald turned and there it was behind him, a yellow glow. Harald looked at the light and the only thing he could make out was "M... Mother...".

CHAPTER 7
SHINING LIGHT

Harald could see it clearly in front of him, the figure of Ingrid was clear and shining before his eyes. "My son, I miss you," said the light to Harald. He fell down with his eyes locked on the beam and the tears started to fall "Mom..." is all he could get out.

The beam of light moved towards Harald and an arm figure came forward and lay on his shoulder and the light transformed into Ingrid's body sitting in front of Harald who was still sitting on the floor untouched. "How are you my son?" asked Ingrid. "Mom is that really you?" Harald answered with a question. "Where are you?" he said again before Ingrid could say anything, he jumped on the beam of light and tried to hug it with his eyes full of tears but his body just went through the beam of light. "I've missed you my dear, I wish I could hug you one last time" continued Ingrid. Harald could not stop his tears, "Stop crying my hero" said Ingrid with a sad face. "Is it really you mom or am I seeing visions?" Harald said in a sad voice. "I had to come and see you one last time my son" answered Ingrid, "I'm here to tell you something important so you must listen to me quickly because I don't know how long I can stay my love" said Ingrid quickly and looked at Harald, "We don't have much time...". Harald raised his face and looked thoughtfully at Ingrid with a confused expression. Ingrid floated towards the rocking chair and sat down, looking at Harald who continued to sit down on the floor and look at her.

"Three centuries ago, we humans on this earth lived a completely different life," Ingrid began to tell. "We lived a life full of consumption and selfishness where everyone thought of their own good. We hardly had any friends and the family relationship was of no importance. We consumed more than we could generate and several people died of starvation and no access to clean water and healthcare. The only thing people cared about was themselves," Ingrid continued to tell, she also told about how the war started and how most of the people were wiped out.

"Our ancestors were alive when the judgment day happened, what they knew but no one believed was that the first atomic bomb that was dropped was a plan to start a war between all the great powers, the plan was to exterminate us humans from this earth." Ingrid told Harald who sat there stunned by it.

"Before we were wiped out, our ancestors asked the earth to stop exterminating us and that we humans can change to give us one last chance. Earth agreed and gave us one last chance where we have to prove that we can change and then New Valhalla was born as an oasis for us humans where there is no prejudice, where everyone thinks of each other and there is no place for selfishness. However, the earth chose to create a counterforce and let other people live to create a counterforce."

"Lagos was created as an antithesis to New Valhalla and then several of us who went back to old habits started moving there to live the way we lived before. We tried to create a community where we show people the value of community but no matter what we did, all our attempts failed."

"Our ancestors then decided to use their greatest gift which is their faith to convince everyone of the importance of this, so the others used their gift to obscure this by tempting people to be selfish and care more about themselves than his fellow men."

"The gift you have my son can change their behavior and make them go back to the way of our ancestors. Go there my son, help the people to go back to the right path...".

Harald sat completely silent and surprised by Ingrid's words and tried to grasp what she was explaining. Before he could say a word, Ingrid suddenly turned her face and took on a more serious expression. She slowly turned her face towards Harald and said "Now I must go again, but never forget that my heartbeat will always be among yours. It will always accompany you on the road no matter which road you take." she got a smile on her face and tears in her eyes and continued "I wish I could have seen your greatness my son, to be by your side, but no matter what happens, I will always be by your side". Harald looked dejectedly at Ingrid with tears in his eyes and could say "Mother. I love you!". Ingrid disappeared.

CHAPTER 8
TO LAGOS

Harald was woken up by Gjør's roar from behind the door, which is called that it is time to go hunting. Harald ran towards the door to meet Gjør whose expression changed instantly when he saw Harald's expression and could only say "Has something happened brother?". Harald could only stare at Gjør and say "I have to go to Lagos". The friends stood still and just looked at each other in silence.

Gjør sat on the couch while Harald told about everything that happened, from the heartbeat in the Storskogen to Ingrid's light during the night. He just sat quietly and listened to Harald who used to never be so confused and determined at the same time.

After Harald finished, he looked at Gjør expectantly to hear his opinion. Gjor glanced at the rocking chair and then he quickly got up and said "Then we're going to Lagos".